How the Dinosaurs Disappeared

Harold G. Kelly

The Rosen Publishing Group's

READING ROOM
Collection: Science™

New York

Published in 2006 by The Rosen Publishing Group, Inc.
29 East 21st Street, New York, NY 10010

Book Design: Haley Wilson

Photo Credits: Cover, pp. 1, 2–3, 7, 14–15, 16 © Kevin Schaffer/ Allstock; pp. 4, 12 © Jim Zuckerman/Corbis; p. 8 © Corbis/ Bettman; p. 11 © PhotoDisc.

ISBN: 1-4042-3340-7

Library of Congress Cataloging-in-Publication Data

Kelly, Harold G. (Harold Greg), 1968-
How the dinosaurs disappeared / Harold G. Kelly.-- 1st library ed.
 p. cm. – (Rosen Publishing Group's reading room collection.
   Science)
Includes index.
ISBN 1-4042-3340-7 (library binding)
1. Dinosaurs--Extinction--Juvenile literature. 2. Reptiles, Fossil–
Juvenile literature. I. Title. II. Series.
QE861.6.E95K45 2006
567.9--dc22
                                              2005011883

Manufactured in the United States of America

Contents

The Dinosaurs

Dinosaurs were animals that lived millions of years ago. Some dinosaurs looked a lot like the **reptiles** that live today, such as lizards, crocodiles, and snakes. Many different kinds of dinosaurs lived for about 150 million years all over Earth. Then they died.

The dinosaurs disappeared from Earth about 65 million years ago.

What Is a Fossil?

When dinosaurs died, mud and sand covered their bodies. Over millions of years, the mud, sand, bones, and teeth became rock. These rocks are called **fossils**. Today, **scientists** study fossils to find out when dinosaurs lived and why they died.

Scientists have discovered fossils from more than 450 different kinds of dinosaurs.

7

How Did the Dinosaurs Die?

Scientists have two main ideas about how the dinosaurs died. One idea is that a change in Earth's weather killed the dinosaurs. The winters became too cold, and the summers became too hot. The seas may have dried up. The dinosaurs could not have **survived** these changes.

It is possible that changes in Earth's weather killed the dinosaurs.

A Rock from Space

Scientists also believe that a **meteor** from space crashed into Earth about 65 million years ago. When the meteor hit Earth, it sent big clouds of dust into the air. Heat from the crash may have started huge fires. The dust and smoke blocked out sunlight for months all over Earth.

When you see a shooting star in the night sky, you are really seeing a meteor.

The Dinosaurs Had No Food

Without sunlight, Earth became very cold. Plants could not grow. Plant-eating dinosaurs may have died because they didn't have any food. Meat-eating dinosaurs needed plant-eating dinosaurs for most of their food. Without plant-eating dinosaurs, meat-eating dinosaurs would have had little food to eat.

 Dinosaurs like this one may have died because there was very little food for them to eat.

The End of the Dinosaurs

Birds and **mammals** could survive the cold because they had feathers or fur to keep them warm. They could eat seeds, nuts, and dead plants to stay alive. Dinosaurs had no way to keep warm. There was not enough food for them to eat. The dinosaurs disappeared from Earth.

Glossary

fossil   A rock formed from the bones of animals or parts of plants that were once alive.

mammal   A warm-blooded animal that is often covered with hair or fur.

meteor   A rock from space.

reptile   A cold-blooded animal that is usually covered with scales, such as a crocodile, a lizard, or a snake.

scientist   A person who studies the way things are and how they act.

survive   To stay alive.

Index